This book belongs to

_____

Jan 2002

HAPPY BIRTHDAY
Luc

A READ-ALOUD STORYBOOK

Adapted by Ron Fontes and Justine Korman

MOUSE WORKS

Find us at www.DisneyBooks.com for more Mouse Works fun!

Printed in the United States of America.

ISBN 0-7364-0120-2

THE BIRTHDAY PARTY

"**R**each for the sky! You're going to jail, one-eyed Bart!" cried Andy.

Then Andy pulled the string and Woody said, "You're my favorite deputy." The brave cowboy was Andy's favorite toy.

3

Andy's mom called from downstairs, "Okay, birthday boy. Go get your sister. It's almost time for your party."

When Andy left the room, his toys came to life!

"Pull my string! The birthday party's today," Woody exclaimed, jumping up. "Okay, everybody, it's clear!"

4

Andy had many toys: Hamm the piggy bank, Rex the timid dinosaur, Bo Peep and her sheep, the Green Army Men, RC the radio-controlled car, and more!

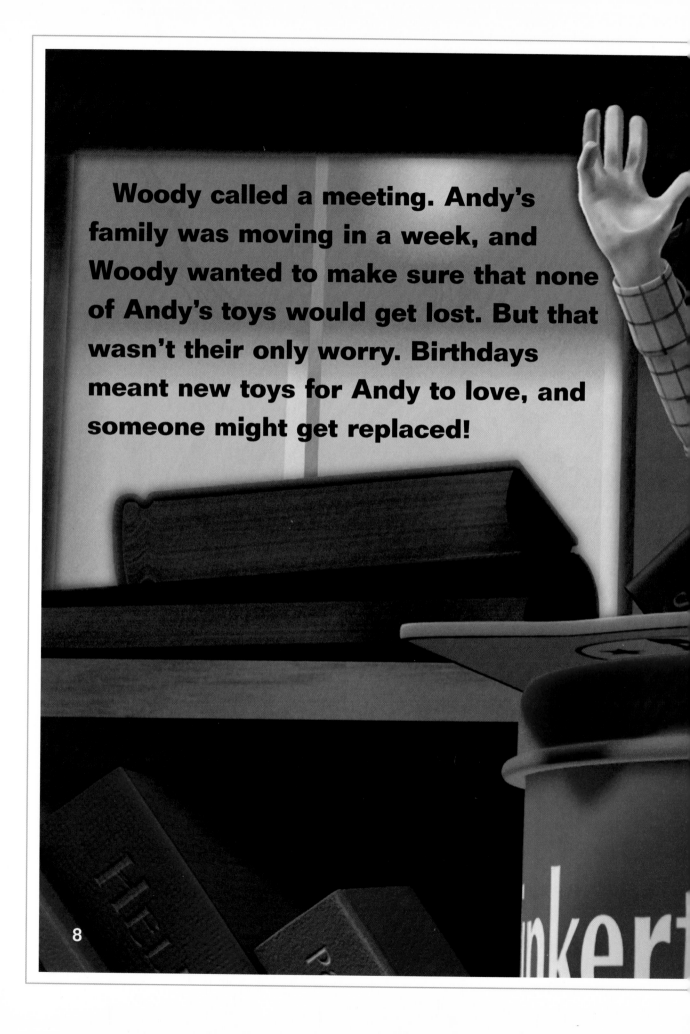

Woody called a meeting. Andy's family was moving in a week, and Woody wanted to make sure that none of Andy's toys would get lost. But that wasn't their only worry. Birthdays meant new toys for Andy to love, and someone might get replaced!

Woody sent the Green Army Men to spy on the birthday party. The sergeant said, "Code red, men. Recon plan Charlie. Move!"

The soldiers reported that Andy got a lunch box, bedsheets, and a board game. The toys cheered!

"Nothing to worry about," said Woody.
Then Andy's mom brought out a
surprise present!

"It's a huge package . . . it's a . . . "
Before the sergeant could finish his
report, Andy and his friends raced up to
his room. The toys froze.

14

Andy tossed his new toy on the bed—in Woody's spot! The cowboy fell to the floor. Then the children left to play games.

Woody dusted himself off and told the other toys, "Let's give whatever it is up there a nice, big, Andy's room welcome."

The new toy was Buzz Lightyear, space ranger! He came in a fancy box shaped like a spaceship.

Buzz activated his wrist-communicator and said, "Buzz Lightyear to Star Command, come in. Do you read me?"

Buzz thought he'd crash-landed on a strange planet. When Woody greeted the new arrival, Buzz fired his laser at the "alien."

"Whoa! I didn't meant to frighten you," Woody said. "I'm Woody and this is Andy's room. And there's been a bit of a mix-up—the bed is *my* spot."

The other toys crept up on the bed. They were impressed by Buzz. "He's got more gadgets on him than a Swiss Army knife," said Bo Peep.

"You're just a toy. T-O-Y," Woody explained to Buzz. "Your laser is just a blinky light and you can't fly."

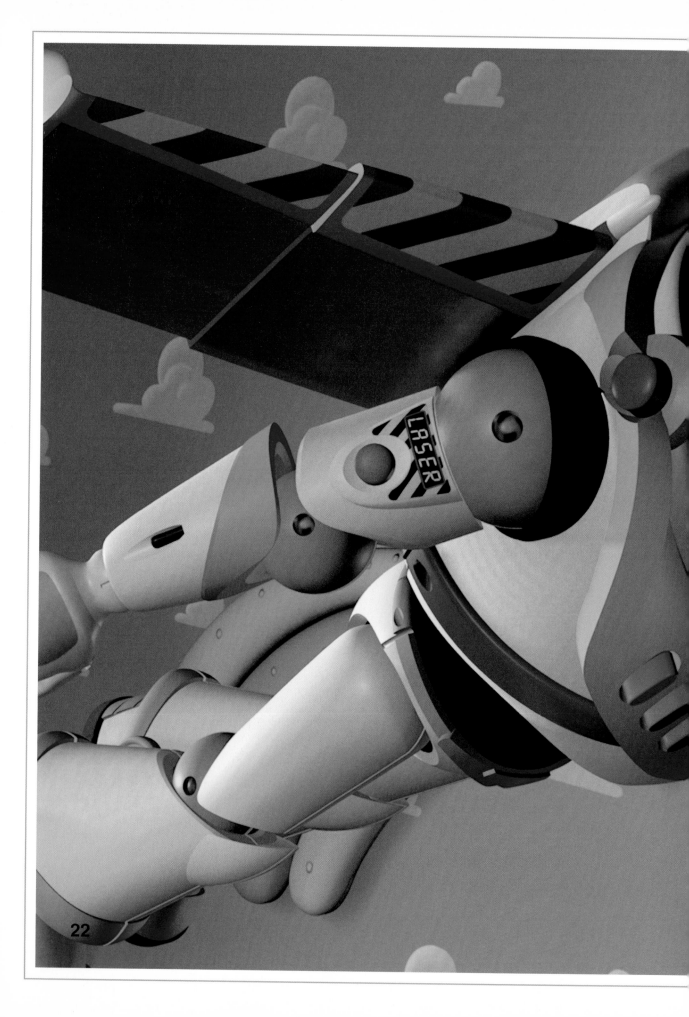

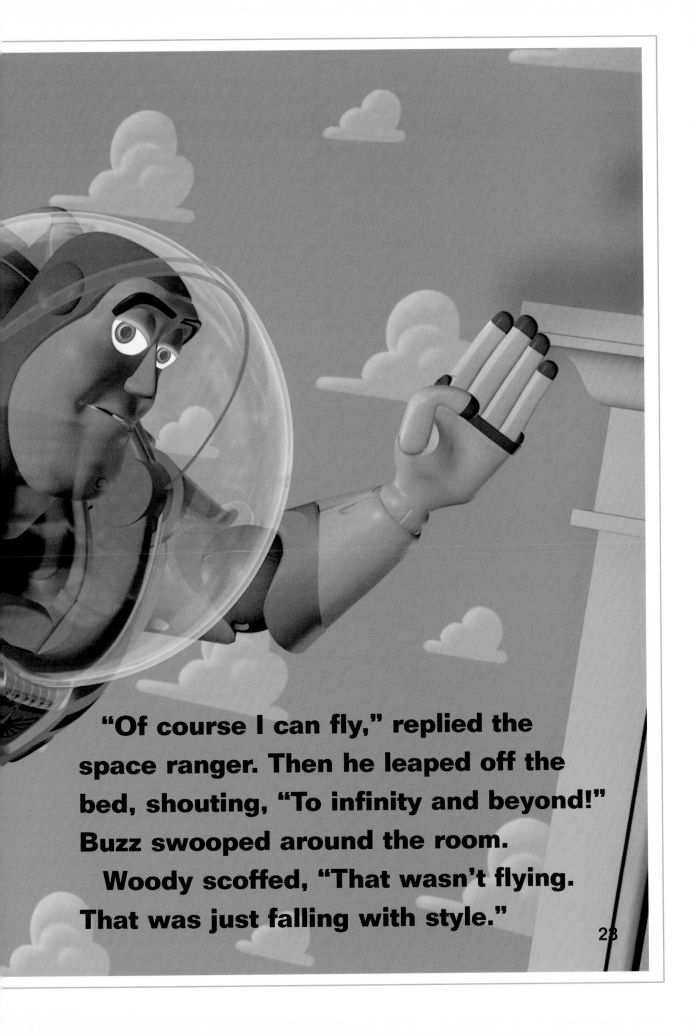

"Of course I can fly," replied the space ranger. Then he leaped off the bed, shouting, "To infinity and beyond!" Buzz swooped around the room.

Woody scoffed, "That wasn't flying. That was just falling with style."

LOOK OUT FOR SID!

One day, the toys heard a cruel laugh. They looked next door and saw Sid, Andy's mean neighbor, blowing up a toy soldier.

"What's going on?" Buzz wondered.

"Sid tortures toys just for fun!" Rex explained.

Later Andy's mom told Andy it was time for dinner at Pizza Planet—and Andy could bring only one toy. Woody wanted to be that toy, so he tried to push Buzz behind the desk. But Buzz wound up falling out the window!

The other toys were angry at Woody's careless prank.

Andy couldn't find Buzz, so he took Woody. But Buzz managed to scramble into the car, too.

"You're alive! I'm saved," Woody cried.

Woody couldn't wait to bring Buzz home to prove that he wasn't a villain. But at Pizza Planet, Buzz saw a spaceship and rushed inside. The spaceship was really a claw game full of alien toys.

Woody tried to get Buzz out, but it was too late! Someone was already working the game's claw.

"Gotcha!" cried Sid, as he plucked a tiny alien.

Then Sid pulled out the space ranger! Woody struggled to save Buzz, but wound up getting pulled out of the spaceship, too.

"Awright! Double prizes!" Sid crowed. "Let's go home and play." Sid had a scary gleam in his eyes.

Sid's room was a nightmare of mangled, mutant playthings. Woody and Buzz watched in horror as Sid's dog, Scud, chewed on the tiny alien. Then Sid "operated" on his sister's favorite doll.

"I am outta here!" Woody cried.

Buzz and Woody tried to escape. But Scud was sleeping in front of the door. Suddenly, the dog woke up!

While Scud chased the toys, Woody hid in the closet.

At that moment, Buzz saw a Buzz Lightyear commercial on TV. Now Buzz knew the truth: he *was* a toy!

The space ranger tried one last time to fly, but ended up at the bottom of the stairs with his left arm broken. Dejected, he didn't even care when Sid's sister dressed him up for her tea party.

As soon as the little girl left her room, Woody rushed to Buzz's rescue. "You've had enough tea. Let's get out of here," he said.

Buzz moaned, "I'm a sham. I can't even fly out the window."

"Out the window! Buzz, you're a genius!" Woody exclaimed. He threw a string of Christmas lights from Sid's window to Andy's. They were saved!

But the toys in Andy's room remembered that Woody had made Buzz fall out the window. They weren't about to help a villain. They dropped the lights.

Back in Sid's room, the mutant toys had just
fixed Buzz's arm when Sid came in the room
with a fireworks rocket. He strapped it to Buzz!
Luckily the launch was delayed by rain.

Sid grinned. "Tomorrow's forecast: sunny."
Buzz was doomed!

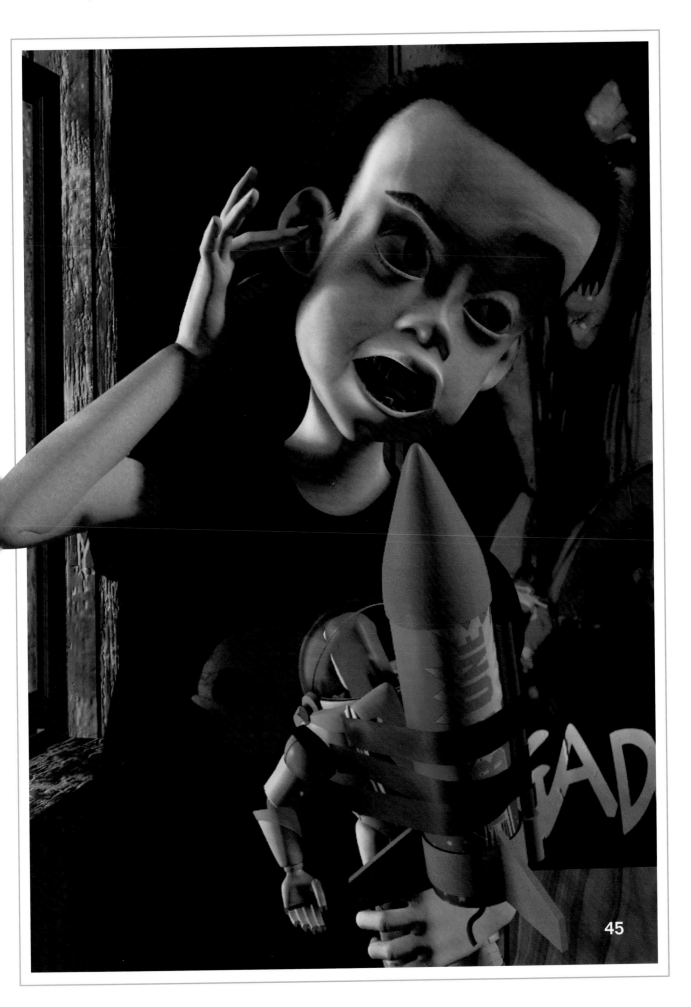

BLAST OFF!

After Sid went to bed, Woody called out, "Buzz, I need you!" Woody was trapped under a crate.

"I can't help," Buzz replied. "I'm just a toy."

"Any toy would give up his moving parts just to be you!" Woody said. "Andy thinks you're the greatest!"

Buzz thought about Andy and the fun they'd had. "Let's go. There's a kid who needs us."

Just as Buzz freed Woody, Sid woke up! "Time for liftoff!" Sid yelled, and he took Buzz outside.

"There's a good toy out there that's going to be blown to bits. We've got to help him!" Woody told the mutant toys. "Please."

Following Woody's plan, the toys took positions in Sid's backyard.

Sid picked up a match to light Buzz's rocket and started the countdown.

51

Just as the match touched the fuse, Sid
heard someone say, "Reach for the sky!" Sid
turned in surprise. Woody was talking, but he
hadn't pulled the toy's string!

"I'm talking to you, Sid," Woody told the
surprised boy. "We don't like being blown up
or smashed or ripped apart."

"W-w-w-we?" Sid gasped.

"Your toys," Woody replied.

The mutant toys moved in on their former tormentor, and Sid ran screaming into his house.

Woody thanked the mutant toys. Then he heard Andy's mother say, "Bye, house." Andy's family was moving!

Buzz and Woody watched as Andy's car drove away.

Pursued by Scud, Woody and Buzz ran to catch the moving van. To save Woody, Buzz jumped onto Scud's nose. Now Woody was safely on the van, but Buzz was left behind on the street!

Woody dug RC out of a box and tossed the radio car onto the street. He could use RC to bring Buzz back. But the other toys still thought that Woody had betrayed Buzz. They threw Woody off the truck!

Then the toys saw Buzz in the street. "Woody was telling the truth," said Bo Peep. The toys watched as Woody, Buzz, and RC raced toward the van.

But RC's batteries ran down! Suddenly, Buzz had an idea. "The rocket!"

Woody used Buzz's helmet to focus sunlight, and fired up the rocket's fuse.

FOOSH! The sizzling rocket soared into the sky! Woody managed to drop RC into the van.

"Hey, Buzz, you're flying." Woody laughed.

"I'm just falling with style," Buzz replied, smiling.

"Uh, Buzz? We missed the truck," Woody pointed out.

"We're not aiming for the truck," Buzz said, diving into the car. The toys landed in the box next to Andy!

After that, all was well in Andy's new home—until Christmas, which meant new toys. On Christmas Day, the anxious toys listened to the Green Army Men's report.

"You aren't worried, are you?" Woody teased Buzz. "What could Andy possibly get that is worse than you?"

From downstairs came the sound of barking. Andy happily exclaimed, "Wow! A puppy!"